All the World's a Page

A Shakespearean Sonnet-Inspired Anthology
by Various Authors from Across the Globe

QUILLKEEPERS PRESS

ISBN: 978-1-969601-00-2

Published by Quillkeepers Press, LLC
PO Box 10236
Casa Grande, AZ 85130

Dear Reader,

Thank you for joining us on this journey through the timeless realm of the Shakespearean sonnet.

At Quillkeepers Press, we believe the sonnet is one of poetry's most exquisite architectures. Its fourteen-line form, wrapped in rhythm, argument, and emotional turn, invites the poet to distill complexity into something elegantly contained. We imagine you feel the same, considering you've found your way here.

As you move through this anthology, you may notice variations in spelling, punctuation, and stylistic choices— American and British English, traditional and contemporary inflections, classical and innovative rhythms. We have preserved these differences with care. They reflect the rich diversity of voices within this collection, and honoring each poet's intention felt essential to the integrity of the work.

Our hope is that within these sonnets you discover resonance, surprise, and a renewed appreciation for what the form can hold.

With Love and Care.

Stephanie Lamb, EIC
Quillkeepers Press

Contents

Alexis Barton   11

   Advice for a Lover   12

Linda Conroy   13

   For the Cherry Trees   14

   Where Once Were Trees   15

Sharron Green   16

   The Company of Thought   17

   Buried Treasure   18

   Waxing Lyrical   19

   Sonnet to do   20

   Wild Swimming in a Scottish Pool   21

Jeffrey Beck   22

   Upon Golden Morn with Loyal Friend   23

Lora Butcher   24

   Bright Relief   25

   Then What Becomes the Mind All Bound in Chains   26

Thomas Koron   27

   I Wrote My Lonely Verse Upon a Page   28

   Life Poses Problems   29

   Forever in My Heart   30

James Bellanca   **31**

   A Mother's War Spoils   32

   Kissing in the Rain   33

Michele Harvey   **34**

   We Bid Farewell   35

   The Red One   36

Bob Lewis   **37**

   Museum   38

   On the occasion of my birth   39

   Determinism   40

   Householder   41

   Klimt   42

Lisa Montagne, Ed.D.   **43**

   Fearlessness   44

Herman Wilkins   **45**

   A Proposal in Times of Forbidden Love   46

Nigel   **47**

   No Holds Bard #1   48

   No Holds Bard #4   49

Kris Michelle Diesness   **50**

   I Watch the Clouds That Float Inside My Eye   51

   A Passion Stirs Beneath the Shroud of Sleep   52

   Your Soured Words Infest My Mind With Flies   53

   When Muses Cue a Kindling of the Art   54

   Passion's Envy, Reason's Pure Delight   55

Melanie Perish   **56**

    Leaf, Wing, and Memory   57

    When Time and Travel Slow   58

    Thanksgiving Again   59

Zenobia   **60**

    Love Came When I Did Not Expect It   61

    Holding on to a Dream   62

    21st Century Beasts   63

Liam Boyle   **64**

    Apartment   65

    Patrick and Coroticus   66

Patrick Trombly   **67**

    The Ballad of Jimmy J   69

    The Return of Jimmy J   70

Gordan Struić   **72**

    Digital Sonnet   73

    Sonnet of Silence   74

Jamey Hecht   **75**

    Pyro   76

    Too Soon?   77

    Courtly Love at Happy Hour   78

Leslie Hodge   **79**

    The Twilight Years   80

Lao Rubert   **81**

    Bereft   82

John Robinson 83

 Keats 84

Violet-May Davey 85

 Can Opposites Really Attract? 86

Estelle Tudor 87

 Fae Sonnet 88

Leanne Moden 89

 Fen Vixen 90

 Ecdysis 91

 Creation With an Axe 92

Rohan Buettel 93

 The Dolphin 94

 The Green Parasol 95

Gerburg Garmann 96

 Avian Vestiges 97

 The Golden Swarm 98

 Twilight's Breath 99

Edward Heathman 100

 California King Bed 101

Deborah Ketai 102

 Chamber Music 103

 4 a.m. 104

Valerie Little 105

 Classify 106

Mark Andrew Heathcote   **107**

   Bleary-eyed beauty   108

Vaishnavi Pusapati   **109**

   Of Light and Dark   110

   Betwixt Dreams and Daylight   111

David Ram   **112**

   Broad Brook Basin   113

   Hockey Jersey 18   114

   Public Skating   115

Ben Goldnagl   **116**

   Appendix C   117

Joshua Walker   **118**

   For Love, I Laid My Sword Beside the Flame   119

Lynn D. Gilbert   **120**

   Cassandra's Complaint   121

Vanessa Caraveo   **122**

   The Sun's Goodbyes   123

   A Seashore Sonnet   124

Najka Altazy   **125**

   Jam Session   126

Erica Berquist   **127**

   Photinus macdermotti   128

Caidan Walker   **129**

   The Coin of Apocalypse   130

Heidi Joffe — 131

Old World Cuckoo — 132

Numerology of 14 — 133

On Assassins — 134

Rajeshwar Prasad — 135

Screen Shadows — 137

LaVern Spencer McCarthy — 138

In This Land — 139

Frank J. Albert — 140

What to Make of Time — 141

Janice Katz — 142

Perpetual Eclipse — 143

Aims and Ends — 144

R.J. Breathnach — 145

A Sonnet on Betrayal — 146

A.C. Blake — 147

The Reader Who Stays — 148

Subhashree — 149

A Sonnet for My City — 150

Ellen Harrold — 151

Streetlight — 152

Logan McDermott-Mostowy — 153

perennial (sonnet for a spring morning) — 154

Sally Mills — 155

The Observer — 156

Shreya 157

    Sonnet 401(k): The Cost of Living 158

Susan Irvine 159

    Snatch Fire 160

    I loved you 161

Paul Burgess 162

    The Darkling Thrush's Ear 163

Elaine Desmond 164

    Golden 165

Damaris West 166

    Penumbra 167

Beth Kanell 168

    Visiting the House of Robert Frost— and His Wife Elinor 169

    Yankee Girl 170

Alexis Barton is a poet and student from Woodstock, GA. Her work can be found in *Sheepshead Review*, *The Journal of Undiscovered Poets*, *The Listening Eye*, and more, and her debut poetry collection is set to be published by Dipity Press by the end of 2025. She works as a poetry reader for *Chestnut Review* and attends Kennesaw State University to become an editor. In her spare time, she enjoys baking macarons, drinking coffee, and watching the rain. Instagram:@alexisinink

Advice for a Lover

A light turns on ahead, leaves us standing

alone we wait for good things to follow;

our hearts have us falling without landing,

when did love become a thing so hollow?

Our promises fade like fire into dust

we let them sink too far beneath the waves;

if love becomes a power lacking trust,

why do we act like it always behaves?

Yet, that light keeps shining to guide us back

and we hold it dearer than we let know;

so, if true love is something that we lack,

we should dig deep and find how to let go.

The true love we know is somewhere inside

we just have to let go instead of hide.

Linda Conroy is a retired social worker who likes to write about the complexities of human nature, our connection with the natural world, and to the changing times. Her poems have been published widely, and she is the author of two poetry collections, *Ordinary Signs* and *Familiar Sky*.

For the Cherry Trees

Exploding into brightness every spring

your blossoms glow and shake with spume,

and though I love to see a pretty thing,

I worry that some petals fail to bloom.

If weather's ways are to be understood,

I watch pinks tumble in light rain, blow down,

are spilled, squashed, trampled, trod in mud,

before a fullness reaches their true crown.

However, since it's pointless to ask why

when nature gives as freely as it takes,

I'd best let go of questioning the sky,

show sympathy with nature's cyclic fates.

Enjoy what is, for spring will come again

and I won't mind if I must wait 'til then.

Where Once Were Trees

Cement, high-rises, with big trucks and buses,

dead leaves, daisies in the sidewalk cracks,

with dirt, debris, with banging, errant fusses,

the shouting of the news, the latest rap.

Quick tap of shoes, of nails, of walking sticks,

stains of oil, of grease, of mud, of paint.

Newspapers torn and trampled on wet bricks,

ticking meters, neon lights, for traffic's plaint

the sirens, mice and beetles, rats, and drains,

moss, mold and spillage, dirt and mildew,

ladders, awnings, pilings, hoardings, trains

in stations. People waiting, needing rescue,

sleep in alleys, crawl through windows,

hold their tears, as day comes to a close.

Sharron Green is a fan of rhyming poetry forms and has included a number in her pamphlets. Some were discovered via challenges on Instagram, where she is known as @rhymes_n_roses. Her latest chapbook, Rhymes for the Mind, contains five sonnets and 'Sonnet to Do' has been selected to appear in this year's *Morecambe Poetry Festival Anthology*. Sharron's work blends nostalgia, nature and comments on modern life. A confident and skilled performance poet, she co-hosts open-mic poetry nights and is a member of the Booming Lovelies, a trio of poets who perform at festivals around Surrey and London.

The Company of Thought

I never feel alone when I am thinking,

the waves just ebb and flow inside my head.

They sometimes shock, unblock or jog some inking

as I cling on, exploring every thread.

Bleak themes attract me back to gawp, like crime scenes.

'What ifs?' are often pondered, plots are changed.

I analyse what each twist of the knot means—

but it's no more than deckchairs rearranged.

And finding fault of course is where I linger,

my fingers tracing contours, pressing sores.

Exhausted, all my choices face the wringer,

I struggle to keep tally of my flaws.

Walls of my mind replastered and repainted

help me and calm become better acquainted.

Buried Treasure

Memories leak from your cotton wool mind.

Curdle cream flotsam sinks quick into sand.

Facts at your fingertips you used to find,

now out of reach, cordoned off, contraband.

Faces approach with familiar tone

relish referring to recent events

claim they're related to youngsters you've known—

why all the questions that do not make sense?

Let's take a wander down well-trodden paths,

tour of the highlights of life lived so well,

titbits of sadness merge with love and laughs

conjured by images, music and smell.

You're not the you that you used to be

that's why I treasure rare glimpses I see.

Waxing Lyrical

Champagne a summer cyclone sceptered isle

Dream shards of slithered serpents in the sun

Scale cotton clouds and snuggle in their pile

Bounce in a rainbow castle, just for fun

Charm bracelets jostling to spill their souls

Ride rockets through the universe to peace

Stretch into child's pose o'er burning coals

Hide 'til the Sevillana's strut swirls cease

Meringue, a melody with lemon zest

Knit, crochet and cross stitch to pass the time

Dew drop a syllable, refresh your nest

Sing sonnets serenading summit's climb

If breathing starts to trouble you, relax

Then dip your finger into molten wax

Sonnet to do

I take a stroll in shade and shelter,

from the weather's wild affray.

The gutsy dog with rusty pelt, a

panting partner, plots the way.

Through tangled yews strewn yesteryear

our steps peruse the path.

Distilling clues, ferns gesture near,

a cleansing nature bath.

So, to the meadow's pulsing lifeline,

shiver grass and bumble,

we saunter home re-tuned, in chime,

from bigger picture, humble.

The daily walk, sometimes a chore,

reveals fresh pastures to explore.

Wild Swimming in
a Scottish Pool

No time to dither, just slip in

and feel the rush of cold to heart.

The tingle ripple on the skin

as tadpoles dash and skaters dart.

Imagine snakes and pirate bones,

'neath murky water mottled green.

Tread water or else toe the stones,

keep mouth clenched tight and drink the scene.

A swooping swallow bids hello

whilst midges gather busily,

the newts are partying below,

like butterflies you're floating free.

Once out, invigoration burns

to jump back in the body yearns.

Jeffrey Beck is a retired Army soldier and a graduate student in the MFA program at Southern New Hampshire University. He earned his BA in English, summa cum laude, from American Military University. He lives with his wife on a five-acre homestead in southern Virginia, where he enjoys tending chickens, reading, and writing fiction, fantasy, and poetry. He is currently at work on a memoir about his combat experience in Iraq.

Upon Golden Morn with Loyal Friend

I seek the morn and the golden dew wide

Your joyous clamor greets the sultry sun

You have spent your life loyal at my side

And that has made e'vry hour a better one

Graciously, your tail beats songs of delight

Is your aim affection? I know, I am sure

Your dash to catch a toy in fading flight

And your wagging joy is the sweetest cure

While royals brag of jewels so rich and rare

And warriors prize the scars of bitter war

My fortune lies within your tender stare

Your love is a tale of Labrador lore

    As long as I must draw this mortal breath

    My heart is yours until we part by death

Lora Butcher won first place in Chorus Of Selves, by Wingless Dreamer, for her flash fiction; second place for poetry in the Bright Star Award 2024, and second place in the Brick by Lego Brick contest 2025 of the Poetry Society of Indiana. She has work forthcoming in *Orchards Poetry Journal; Cryptids` Kaiju & Corn*, from Midwest Press, and *Yellow: A Hue Are You* anthology from Jambu Press. She has been published in *The Hedge Apple Literary Magazine; Chaos, Crisis, and Conflict,* by Moonstone Press; *The Heartland Review; Ink To Paper Vol. 8 & 9;* and *The Lyric*. She leads a local chapter of Shut Up & Write.

Bright Relief

There came the sun above her drooping grief.

A melody of thought that sang in dreams

Began to bloom in notes of bright relief

That rang along the banks of sacred streams.

She felt the hymns of old were there in forms

That hide among the wild circumstance

Of life some call a wilderness. What warms

The senses to goodwill, the silver chance

To find the hope she needs to love, to know

Above the bitterness of life's defeat

That tells her to pursue the peace, the glow

Within continuums that do repeat

The ancient ways redeeming all the pain

With wonderland and paradise regain.

Then What Becomes the Mind
All Bound in Chains

Then what becomes the mind all bound in chains,

Who freedom wants to give another chance?

She comes and lifts her light upon the plains

Of solitude and seas of circumstance.

That even one might raise their head above

What drowns the outreach of the breath and hand

And to the shore of other gently shove

The folded mind until they come to land.

Then like a book they open where they dock

Among potential friends or enemies

And come to deal with the uneven shock

To put away the ax and pick the keys.

Release the chains and open all the doors

To what the Lady Liberty adores.

Thomas Koron was born in Grand Rapids, Michigan on May 19, 1977. He has attended Grand Rapids Community College, Aquinas College, Western Michigan University, Northern Illinois University and the American Conservatory of Music. His previous literary projects include poetry, stage plays, short stories, and a novel. He currently lives in the Chicago metropolitan area.

I Wrote My Lonely Verse Upon a Page

I wrote my lonely verse upon a page,

As I kept working late into the night.

Traveling down a desolate passage,

With inspiration as my only light.

As you graded each paper in the pile,

You stayed awake through the late evening hours.

Hard-working students always made you smile,

When they showed you their musical powers.

A dark room revealed the light in your eyes,

As you came up to me in slow motion.

Quickly feeling the warmth of the room rise,

We were both overcome with emotion.

At last, we had found an undying love,

Reminding us of the gift from above.

Life Poses Problems

Life poses problems that we all must solve,

Each time that challenging moments occur.

Together, new directions that involve

Less effort causes old problems to deter.

On days when it seems that there is nothing

Valuable to be found to ease the pain,

Endurance is what is needed to bring

Peace of mind back into life once again.

Recurrent thoughts of you cure my despair

Every moment we find ourselves apart.

Vanquishing sorrow I once had to bear,

And reviving solace within my heart.

In my sleep, I dreamt of your countless charms,

Longing to one day hold you in my arms.

Forever in My Heart

Forever in my heart and on my mind,

Over the course of time, this was written.

Recalling each of the pure and refined

Memories of when I became smitten.

Your presence brought newfound joy to my life

During a time when I felt most forlorn.

Ending years of bitter heartache and strife,

As a beautiful romance was soon born.

Reverently in silence, my sincere

Love for you kept growing with persistence.

Under the surface, I held you most dear,

Captivated by your mere existence.

    Inside my heart something had awoken,

    All the time things were felt, but not spoken.

James Bellanca, a novice poet, a retired English teacher, and lifelong gardener, composes poems about his garden, environmental sustainability, social justice, climate change, peace, family, love, grief, and senior life. He prefers metaphor, allusion, and story in a variety of forms, especially sonnets, villainelle, and American cinquain. *The Aeriel Chart. Down In the Dirt, the literary hatchet, Last Leaf, Sparks of Caliope, Westwood Quarterly, The Lyric, 7th Phyric Circle, The Etherial Haunted Journal,* and other publications have accepted his poems. He lives in Lake Forest, Illinois with his wife of 61 years.

A Mother's War Spoils

What is her feeling on this mourning day

when rolling up her blue silk sock as tears

leak down her pallid cheeks? Her sock midway,

she stops. Outside her windowsill, she hears

a robin's chirp, a cheerless last goodbye,

a mother's sigh-filled dirge. She draws a breath.

Her eyes spot sprites pliéing the sky

until one falls, a wounded swam in bloodied dress.

A stolid photo face, no smile, stands guard

on flag bedecking Trident-pinned urns

The mother sinks down on her knees. Her charred

heart speaks no words. Her once dried tears return

to weep *what if?* and *why?* her child was picked

to sacrifice dance-joy to war's death-script?

Kissing in the Rain

How do we hail the days our love has grown

like irises in spring or mums in fall?

These are the times our old folk soul's recall

our love, our windfall memories strong-blown

each day across high vales where edelweiss

encourages love's devotion in each soul.

Like flowers twirled around a spring maypole,

our cherished love entwines our heated bliss.

Now old with six decades of marriage fled,

we talk, remembering how we found small ways

to share our time— by giving hugs each day,

by speaking kind words, sharing dinner chores,

by feeling sorrow for the other's pain,

by kissing soft while dancing in the rain.

Michele Harvey is a poet whose work has appeared in several literary journals including: *Progenitor, Copper Nickel, The Litchfield Review* and in her self-published collection, *Poetry For Living An Inspired Life*

We Bid Farewell

Estate sellers help us unload silver

Wares blotted and tainted now retired

Fluted goblets ring in hands that quiver

Engraved candlesticks shed light without fire

Keepsakes wait baited for strangers to view

Red cases open as bidders march past

Spoons hang sullen like a yellowing moon

Stopwatches mark time from shelves behind glass

A blue-haired man bids on pop's nickel plate

Rust and neglect reflect absent luster

Dark blemishes show time humiliates

Our family's past, sold by slick conductors

Random hands rise like initial scratches

Bids spur high stakes, legacy dispatches

Previously published in Poetry for Living an Inspired Life.

The Red One

Crumbled, dated Lowellian theory—

Strangers from a world, whose veins draw upon

Rivers flowing, toward dry seabeds, dreary

Life amid red rust, perihelion.

New mariners photograph icy clouds.

From a globe sublime, only vapors run.

Dry ice crystals cap, windswept ferrous shrouds.

No silver fluids course canals fine spun.

Only navy sky, soils fitted by seas

Of frozen dust: elliptical reachings—

House the huge shield volcanoes which exceed

Fossils revealing this planet's teachings.

Conjured dreams, ancient life, nomenclature,

Thirst for home of an unearthly nature.

Previously published in Astropoetica, Fighting Chance Magazine, and Poetry for Living an Inspired Life.

Bob Lewis is a retired lawyer, transitioning from Nome, Alaska to Portland, Oregon. He credits his zoom poetry and writing groups (and their wild diversity of thought and experience) with any successes in the submitted lines.

Museum

Sandy half-shells and smooth bright-shining stones

A mason jar contains things left behind.

Dark corners hide the secrets I once owned,

On the closet floor what will they find?

No mystery can finally attach,

But some crumbs and clutter in a drawer.

What silly, moth-dusted meaning might match

Ragged patch-elbowed costumes I once wore?

Fast boot steps echo down a storage hall,

Past glass-jarred shapes, formaldehyde and foul,

Toward doors, outside where dragging bellies crawl

A land burnt sere, and wolfish shadows prowl;

Eyes red-rimmed, cursed carrion-eaters grew,

Midst pap'ry hives, roused wasps and hornets flew.

On the occasion of my birth

Trumpets resounded. Rich hosannahs sung,

With tear-filled voices, flagons raised, we're told

Of touching cannon-fire and banners hung,

Skyrockets sizzling, bursting red and gold.

Princely patrimony o'er lands far-flung,

Borders barren, snow-peaked, stark and cold

Where winds blew cruel and blackened bodies swung

Midst low-slung clouds while closing thunder rolled.

List now: to happy paeans given tongue,

Of landsmen whose fields, brought back to the fold,

And from whose clerics, bells were finely wrung,

No longer needed for enemies of old.

Sharp-eyed sentries, facing north, whom our poets note,

Watch, bright-helmed, high above a deepened castle moat.

Determinism

Where and what began your checkered journey?

Was it your mother's whiskey binge before

Birth on a suddenly empty gurney

Rather than the emergency room floor?

The unemployed smoker's cough that killed

Your grandfather when he was thirty-nine,

Or fear of crystal prophesies fulfilled,

Fated by some intelligent design?

Did microscopic Brownian motion

Heighten out-put of your adrenal gland?

Initiate a homicidal notion?

When does a random thought become long-planned?

Another black-robed judge is trying to instill,

The feckless benefits of disciplined self-will.

Householder

I'd spent the day plumbing the depths of rage,

Ungainly sprawled, my head beneath the sink.

The posture untoward and not befit my age,

But only just to cause my back to kink.

Knuckles scraped and raw I list' the roiling winds

Outside that bode the winter nigh, and curse

Oxidized, cross-threaded joints that bind,

Unyielding, spite the wrenching cries and worse.

If only this bright sun might yet break through

If only stiff, arthritic fingers might...

And not relent and have to just buy new

And not accept the aging household slight.

How many times more, my thoughts despair

Must need I to the hardware store repair?

Klimt

Aspens shiver windless as the autumn wanes

A redbud, rooted, nods amidst the grove;

A marsh nearby, and branches, filled with cranes,

The artist and his wife, limbs interwove.

Prayers unfurled in the stiffening breeze,

Twisted ribbons, uncoiled threads, uncertain signs,

Unwound across beckoning, wandering seas,

Invitations stretched out now in plaintive lines.

Thoughtlessly embraced as passion welled,

What signal blinded moment have they missed?

What singing has the storied tree withheld,

Fall's escape revealed, had they only list?

Memories flee south as crimson birds unfold,

The lovers yet remain, entwined, in gold.

Lisa Montagne, Ed.D. is a writer, editor, college professor, and educational technology specialist from Southern California. Her poetry, fiction, and essays have been published by Daxson Publishing, World Stage Press, LA Poet Society, Running Wild Press, *The Ear, Variant Magazine,* and *LA Art News*, among others. On the mic in Los Angeles and Orange County for the past decade, she is an alumnus of the Yale Writers' Workshop, and an award-winning poetry instructor for the Community Literature Initiative. Her books include *Robot Lover*, and *Red Flags: Tales of Love and Instinct*. *When Anxiety Has Wings and Other Strange Things*, a collection of poems and essays, is coming soon.

Fearlessness

Fearlessness is the chosen goal, you say?

To be without strikes cold in this arch heart.

I fear many things: traffic, tooth decay,

Bears, the acid skin of some men, to start.

And, in the night, stiff straight, I lay awake,

Because it was chasing me. What was? It!

Fear was there. I fold in filled with soul ache

And...I snuggle it close, damned hypocrite.

This is my life, and I am living it.

Day by day by day by day by day by...

Fear is mine. Mine. Fear: my bitch, my trinket.

When the audience is ready to play...

Fear-less-ness, you say? I want fear. I eat

It for breakfast, for ev'ry meal and treat.

Herman Wilkins is a writer and filmmaker who began his artistic journey in the theater and fell in love with nearly every female character in the Shakespearean world. A recovering and evolving screenwriter whose new media, television and film subjects focus on marginalized and feminists figures such as Ada Lovelace, Eugene Bullard, Maria Callas, and Belle Gunness. In addition to writing educational blogpost and columns for StudioBInder.com since 2018, he is a regular contributor to Vocal.com, where his "A Letter to Donald Trump" won 1st Prize. He is also a 2nd Rounder (Finalists) for the 2019 Sundance Sloan Fellowship, a 2011 Finalists for the ABC-Disney Television Writer's Fellowship, and the recipient of The Kauai Writer's Conference Fellowship in 2023. He is currently finishing his first collection of tales and essays from the quarantine, *In The Hush* , and his first novel *The Mercy of Shadows | In the Dark.*

A Proposal in Times of Forbidden Love

[A Sonnet in Tribute and Remembrance of Obergefell vs Hodges]

What are sweet words in times of shadow'd love?

The echoes of heartbeats could not suffice

For the true voice of my beloved should rise above

And our measur'd souls should ne'er attend vice

How should be said what could come natural

In this our cloaked night that befalls us now

Needs must seek a certain place pastoral

So fate may give all that which love allows

For'er a word becomes a new daylight

And night o'er takes what can not be unknown

Turns lustful needs and twilight trysts to right

To nurse instincts moved by affected bones.

But now the time for words intended true

That I cherish, love and want to marry you.

Nigel, as Head of an English Dept, introduced youngsters to Shakespeare for over 20 years, and he has always dabbled in poetry, especially when he ought to be doing something else. He is bending the rules here, too, but then fun often does —as the trio in Shakespeare's sonnets found...

No Holds Bard #1

A whimsical take on Shakespeare's Sonnets,

his friend and a scholar or two.

If poor teachings made you shrink inside

Whenever Shakespeare's name is said or written,

So that you've never seen the plays, nor tried

To let his sonnets touch and leave you smitten,

Let me attempt seduction with a line

To catch you. Please do review. They're still alive.

Rather than No.1 —try 29,

Then 30, one30 and 65.

You might start wondering Who gave Who a poke.

For those that quote in truly heartfelt way

Shall I compare thee to a summer's day?

Should know those words were spoken to a bloke.

And, always good at flattering his betters,

Shakespeare made his mate a man of letters.

No Holds Bard #4

In several ways conceited, Shakespeare's friend

Was wealthy and deceitful, debonair,

A patronising beauty, fair, unfair.

He twisted Shakespeare's mistress —would she bend?

Yes! Let's drop the old boy off now at Wit's End!

Dark Ladies feel rich boys are there to snare:

Bard's love receded faster than his hair.

Find diamond geezer and his squeezer penned

In poetry, from which there's no release.

We watch the Bard dismantle two affairs

With very different people— equal shares

His teasing us and them will never cease.

How Senioritas turned his "Sir" to "Sirrah"

Thrusts through both love's and words' distorting mirror.

Kris Michelle Diesness resides in Wheaton, Illinois, with her husband and her two cats. She holds a B.A. in English: Writing from Dominican University and an M.A. in Transpersonal Psychology: Spiritual Psychology with Dream Studies Certification from Sofia University. She previously worked for SonnetWriters.com (operational in the mid-2000s), where she contributed original poetry, analytical essays, and the compilation of a metrical dictionary. More recently, two of her poems were featured in *Purr and Yowl: An Anthology of Poetry About Cats* by World Enough Writers.

I Watch the Clouds
That Float Inside My Eye

I watch the clouds that float inside my eye,

pretending hidden portals live within.

Imagine, lands where blindness cannot pry

a book from avid hands devoid of sin.

I offer optic pain as prayerful plea—

my tears a sacrificial wine for sight.

I long to learn why one who begs to see

is called by depths unseen to read and write.

I see the letters sliding off the page,

then vanish into schitic chasms— black.

I lower lids like latches for a cage

and mourn unwritten words the blur holds back.

Yet eyes do not convey the inner sight;

such vision forms my portals every night.

A Passion Stirs Beneath the Shroud of Sleep

A passion stirs beneath the shroud of sleep,

yet sleeps throughout the gleaming hours of sun;

a candle in the dark illumines deep

desires, yet star of daytide shares not one.

While daylight blinds the eye and numbs the depth,

the night awakens blooms from lunar root;

the solar sands ignite a golden debt,

as silver crescent tends the ripest fruit.

With midnight's sweet sepulcher holding dawn

and dusk swirls down reluctant wells of thought,

the senseless reign of tearing fades to gone,

and love will glean the garden sleep once sought.

The waking world appears as hardened clay,

yet dreams reveal the sleeping sides of day.

*Your Soured Words Infest
My Mind With Flies*

Your soured words infest my mind with flies

whose droning quotes your callous tongue with ease.

Their feast, the fetid feces you surmise

and putrid pustules spread by your disease.

Behind my eyes, a swarm of doubts possess—

a buzz like chainsaws mauling Alder groves

that bleed from lesions born from core distress.

Such pestilence infects my hope in droves.

You sculpt your mold and shame me into shape—

your box a rotting coffin built with bile

to force conformity by mental rape,

invalidating my authentic style.

As doubts lie teeming, breeding bugs remain.

Yet Art endures against your pompous stain.

When Muses Cue
a Kindling of the Art

When Muses cue a kindling of the Art

within a space conducive to a slave

as cage of form which threatens to depart

or cacophonic stresses one must stave,

the Tested must resist the urge to waste

away as flames engulf the sullen soul,

confront those mundane demons one had faced

and tame the raging origins 'til they're whole.

As bodies break and burdens tire the mind,

creating soothes the aches of slow decline.

Distractions shatter focus— once refined,

yet Art will seldom hold by planned design.

For Muses gift their graces by decree.

The Art shall guide the Artist to break free.

Passion's Envy,
Reason's Pure Delight

Passion's envy, Reason's pure delight,

the undertaking of a hopeless breed;

No longer feel, embrace the fluid might,

a choice impossible in Thought's own deed.

Break apart the ocean, pour in red,

or float atop the waves far from their depth.

To live and die or live as if now dead

to free the heart of unforeseen torment.

Believe what may be lies or live in doubt,

Shelter's peace or gifts of total Self;

Travel far the mundane, safest route,

or place devotion on the highest shelf.

Live and love and broken you may be,

or shall indifference kill and set you free?

Melanie Perish is a gender-fluid poet who's genetically imprinted to the Sierra Nevada Mountains. Her work has appeared in *Persimmon Tree*, *The Meadow*, *Sequestrum*, *Sinister Wisdom*, *Calyx*, *Abandoned Mine*, and other small press magazines. Her collections include *Passions & Gratitudes* (Black Rock Press, 2011), *The Fishing Poems*, and *Foreign Voices, Native Tongues*. She believes reading makes you beautiful.

Leaf, Wing, and Memory

When green and gray against a vivid blue

can draw my eyes beyond concrete and fence,

the air between takes on a different hue

and shape. Sometimes, both wings and leaves commence

to signal one another's flight. Wings free

to glide, the curved leaf tethered to a lithe

or stalwart branch. It is like memory

these two— a careful pas de deux. In blithe

and gentle winds, the provenance of leaves

belongs to earth and air. Leaves trill or sway

in panacles or rows. Some say it greaves

them just to watch the quick bees fly away

like images in dreams. These flit and go

while leaves and waking thoughts move still and slow.

When Time and Travel Slow

When time and travel find me in one place

Where both have slowed— where I can slip

Away into what's real, I find your face.

Your face, the flesh like mine, lines fine that skip

Your eyes, lake deep. Lines feed like creeks that seek

what's still, what's proud of its own depth. Eyes where

Dark flecks could spin like fallen leaves, could speak

Of surface things or dive deep like trout to share

the swim, the scales, the hidden coves of thought.

Your mouth's not full, but definite with play,

With days talked honestly, with words that ought

And are actions. Your mouth curves deep, a way

of water, speech. When time and travel slow

I find your face— hold what I hold and know.

Previously published in Passions & Gratitudes, Black Rock Press, 2011

Thanksgiving Again

When women come to thank and feast and talk

About the spring's quick brook, the summer's child

The autumn's harvest, Crones begin to walk

Again and plant earth's sleep with myths beguiled

From shooting stars. Crone dreams begin to play

Upon the wind, appear on mountain trees

The ones most near to sunset's fire and gray

Spoked clouds. They rise, unburdened, lift with ease

Like women passing plate and dish and some

Small story in between the slant of sun

And gold-toothed smile. Each year they seem to come

Among us, winning what's already won

Or gleaned from our best selves, I'm told.

Crones feed us with their wit— to have, to hold.

Previously published in Passions & Gratitudes, Black Rock Press, 2011

Zenobia lives in San Antonio, Texas, with her family and loves to disappear into coffee shops and libraries to read and write. She has a collection of poetry, *Survivors of the Sea*, published as part of an anthology called *Black Butterfly: Voices of the African Diaspora*, she has sonnets and a short story published in *Un Poco Rant*, an anthology of Texas writers. Zenobia was recently selected as a finalist for the Dark Poets Prize for "Knock, Knock Anxiety" and was recently published by The Dark Poet's Society. She has a collection of eros inspired poetry in *Neptune Magazine's Nectar Selection: Summer 2025 edition*.

Love Came When I Did Not Expect It

I'd almost forgotten how to breathe in.

My lungs have bloomed roses. My heart is full.

My mouth opens in soft petal yearning.

You knew just how to find the stem and pull—

My red blood returned like sweet air rushing.

I'm not the same, it's like I remember—

Like, how Earth feels still, though we're in spin; but

how did my heart keep heat through dead winter?

This is a miracle. I've kissed kindness.

A once mute sky, now bursts technicolor.

Hours have passed?   I doubt time's existence.

You've split the day's sun —   —moonlight slips faster...

Though these black nights are inevitable,

dawn's halo warms our final parable.

Holding on to a Dream

My heart, soaked in wine, calls for you to come.

I'm lush, a drunk for you but, you've noticed

I'm ocean—

                    peaking past your horizon,

a foam mouthed tide—

        chewing spit-salt surface.

Pain gets too much credit, skip it and dream.

I'd rather we bud fruit, *tart sprouts rising,*

than resentment set our kettles screaming.

In our ritual of snakes and kissing,

night pulls our shadows into one altar.

Sun rises in us, a song summoned call.

The world shakes us awake, my hope slumbers

looking for blooms through holes punched in our walls.

You didn't mean to. . . spackled memory

worn from water, flames and our revelry.

21*st* Century Beasts

When misery holds the day's hour in

a bruise-to-throat, asphyxiating squeeze

my   eyes   sink   back— *oh, black dream horizon*

and imagine hope's second breath of ease.

When did we all become these brutal beasts,

gnashing teeth, foaming on-all-fours, monsters?

Make love to me— a   slow   delicious   feast .

Worship as if we're each other's martyrs.

When the world feels stagnant; you are my breeze,

under pressure, you are treasure beneath.

Heaven is your taste within my tongue's reach;

in a world of want, we   are   all   we   need.

Hope in dark times, *there is never enough.*

We savor each taste, *each sunrise of touch.*

Liam Boyle lives in Galway Ireland. His poetry is mainly focused on memoir and heritage. He is enjoying his retirement and likes to spend time with his grandchildren.

Apartment

As she unwraps herself from lover's limbs,

and quietly slips from bed, rejects its heat,

his breathing stirs, a break in its easy rhythm,

then settles back, resumes a purring beat.

Her mind is restless, busy, sleep has gone.

She pads in darkness to the sitting room

and cracks a curtain, muses idly on

a murky night in concord with her gloom.

In rooms above, below, on either side

her neighbours dream their worries, hopes, and fears,

rekindle memories of love and pride,

revisit loss, perhaps awake in tears.

The clouds pull back, reveal a crescent moon.

She turns for bed, to clasp love in a spoon.

Patrick and Coroticus

(Saint Patrick's letter to the soldiers of Coroticus)

Now roused to rage, he's driven by a wrong

he must call out, in wounded cries of pain

and wrath; the words he chooses, harsh and strong,

protest the slaughter as he mourns the slain.

His converts, freshly baptised, clad in white,

the chrism on their foreheads plain to see,

waylaid and killed, or captured in the fight

to sell as spoils in lands across the sea.

He knows the horror of their plight, his own,

a stranger in a foreign land, a slave.

He calls upon the soldiers to disown

and shun their lord Coroticus, the knave.

Don't fawn or feast this wolfish devil's kin

till he repents and turns away from sin.

Previously published in Causeway/Cabhsair, Volume 13, Issue 2, 2024,

Aberdeen University Press.

Patrick Trombly lives with his partner and stepdaughters in Manhattan. He wrote and published four poems while at Holy Cross, from which he graduated in 1991. Since then, the only poems he wrote, for over 30 years, were sonnets and villanelles for his partner, Corinne. Patrick began writing again in 2025 and took a workshop with Dottie Lasky. He has since submitted poetry for publication, and has already had three poems accepted for publication in 2026. His older stepdaughter graduated from Stuyvesant HS and, before that, from Wagner Middle School. The inspiration for the enclosed sonnets is her classmate and friend Jimmy, who really did sell drugs, and was homeless, yet passed the SHSAT, graduated from Stuy, and attends college, somewhere. That is a very Stuyvesant story. The reference to a Wagner prof is a reference to Ted Boesky. However, it is completely fictional—while Zoe had him as a history teacher. While he was a good teacher, there is zero evidence that he ever had any contact with his

Father's old partners. The poem is a modern, street-smart adaptation of the Biblical story of Joseph and the coat of many colors, and at the same time a take-down of the modern "system." While Patrick believes in hustling and in capitalism and the beneficial end results of it, the idea that our society today is a formal system with any morality to it, and the idea that, to succeed, one must be either moral or chosen, are both absurd. The way up is to hustle. That's great, but let's be honest about it. That is why the hero is a gangster and insider trader —but one who helps his brothers, as Joseph did in the Bible. Note that there is a slight deviation from formal Sonnet structure: an additional stanza. This was needed to further the story. Note that while the story is a ballad, it also fits within the sonnet archetype, because the poem as a whole is a reflection on fate and brotherhood. Yes, the poem is insane. So is NYC. So is society. And we must roll with that, and hustle until we make it. That is the point.

The Ballad of Jimmy J

So much of what is gained starts with a loss.

His folks were married. They named him José.

When they got popped, he escaped to L.A.,

and was brought into our *pandilla* by the Boss.

We thought little of him— a pebble that was tossed.

He rose up the ranks and earned the highest pay.

Boss let him get a tattoo yesterday:

Our snake, but with green feathers— the fuck'd that cost?

That patronizing, no good little fuck—

He played the star, as if we were his cast—

moved too much product, and he moved it too fast.

We black bagged him and put him on a truck,

Sold him to the Eagles gang back East.

They held him down and burned the tattoo off.

They let him live, but now he is their slave.

We blamed it on a narc nicknamed, *'The Beast'*.

We told the Boss that we had fought him off

But that poor Jimmy, we'd tried but failed to save.

The Return of Jimmy J

How long has it been? Fifteen years? Goddam.

Boss made me Captain on that very day,

I told the boys to never mention J.

Then I sold the Boss out to Uncle Sam

And merged us with the Eagles— my payday.

I didn't know I'd end up where I am,

Or that we'd find ourselves stuck in a jam

Because of an ambitious young D.A.

And I didn't know that Jimmy had impressed

The higher ups, who prepped him for the test.

The Eagles weren't just keeping him alive—

He went to school, at Chambers 345.

Then B-school.   Then he took his education

And used it to find and use information

For a fund that knew his prof from junior high.

A stock tip was enough to satisfy

The city cops and keep them off his back.

But he had balls, he wrote calls or went short,

And found rich playboys from whom he could extort,

All while his crew moved truckloads of the crack

That we'd brought cross-country surreptitiously.

The D.A. caught us— offered us a plea.

But Jimmy paid him— got the whole thing tossed.

So much of what is gained starts with a loss.

Ol' Jimmy never did us any harm—

Instead, he welcomed us with open arms.

Gordan Struić is a lawyer, poet, and musician from Zagreb, Croatia. His work has appeared in numerous Croatian and international journals, including *34th Parallel, Half Mystic, Stone Poetry Quarterly, Headlight Review,* and *Poetic Reveries*. In 2025, he received a Special Recognition Award at the Beyond Words contest in Trieste. He writes about silence, memory, and the fragile intersections between loss and renewal.

Digital Sonnet

When silence hums inside a circuit's core,

the ghost of voices lingers in the code.

I type your name, but letters fracture more,

each line corrupted, weighted with the load.

A screen reflects the shadows of my face,

yet hides the pulse that stutters through the wire.

What human warmth can reach this cold-lit space,

when signals fade, consumed by static fire?

The cursor blinks— a clock that will not rest,

a heartbeat mocked by program's rigid law.

It holds the lines my hand could not digest,

unfolding grief in algorithms raw.

Yet still I write, though language seems misplaced:

a sonnet lost, but not yet all erased.

Sonnet of Silence

The room retains the shadow of your breath,

A trace of warmth still clinging to the air.

Each echo lingers, whispering of death,

Yet soft enough to sound as if you care.

The window bends the evening into gray,

A fragile light dissolves upon the floor.

I count the hours you have kept away,

Yet know the silence will withhold much more.

The walls repeat the questions left unsaid,

Their cracks conceal the secrets of our past.

A fragile thread connects the words we shed,

Though none remain resilient to last.

And so I keep this quiet as my own:

A crown of absence, colder than a stone.

Jamey Hecht, PhD, PsyD, LMFT is a psychoanalyst in private practice in Brooklyn, NY. He has a PhD in English and American Literature from Brandeis University (1995), and a Psy.D. in Psychoanalysis from the New Center for Psychoanalysis in L.A. (2019). He has published over a dozen scholarly articles in academic journals of psychology, literary criticism, and the history of ideas, and is the author of five books to date: _Plato's Symposium: Eros and the Human Predicament_ (Twayne, 1999); a translation with commentary, _Sophocles' Three Theban Plays: Antigone, Oedipus the Tyrant, Oedipus at Colonus_ (Wordsworth Editions, 2005); _Bloom's How To Write About Homer_ (Chelsea, 2010); and two books of poetry. _Limousine, Midnight Blue_ (Red Hen Press, 2009) comprises fifty elegies for President Kennedy. Hecht's second poetry collection is _Dodo Feathers: Poems 1989 - 2019_ (International Psychoanalytic Books, 2019).

Pyro

I'll finally admit this, since I'm getting old.

When I was a kid, food stamps bought a brick

of 'Government Cheese': orange, solid, cold.

I covered its scary glow with Ranger Rick

Magazine. A raccoon, with Ranger expertise.

What is government, and how do they turn

it into cheese? I must have tried a piece

and been grossed out. I'd go out back and burn

the cardboard sleeve it came in. Did I know

it meant we were broke? I held the plastic lens

in place, staring at the flame as though

my heart had started it. I guess that depends

on what the poets or psychiatrists decide.

Even at seven, I knew I was too hot inside.

Too Soon?

Marriages? Like chromosomes: too many

screw up everything, but what can you do?

Their promised futures don't add up to any.

They're just there, and now they're part of you.

So many Eleanors Rigby in their homes

(arthritic typists for Attorneys General)

eat Whoppers Junior out of Styrofoam's

chirping toxic convenient shell. Several

poets dead in armchairs undiscovered

for three days have told the world its fate.

Their verses hung in smoke, and hovered

in the dreams of grownups, till the great

north wind blew from the throat of God

the first North Pole monsoon. How odd.

Courtly Love at Happy Hour

Petrarch's Laura, Dante's Beatrice, and you

do brunch, a spa, and Girls' Night Out.

It's Ladies' Night at Billy Shake's, and who

should be behind the bar (to flirt with, shout

at, ogle, take to task for too much ice)

but little Petrarch! Dante sweeps the floor.

I'm in the kitchen, frying your next nice

big plate of fries. Pete pours more

Chardonnay. It happens all the time:

some guy goes crazy, puts a woman

on a pedestal, inside a book: a crime

against her separate Self! She's human.

Look: Bill's ashes on the highest shelf,

and his Dark Lady, drinking by herself.

Leslie Hodge lives in San Diego. Her poems appear in *Catamaran Literary Reader*, *The Main Street Rag*, *South Florida Poetry Journal*, *ONE ART*, *Whale Road Review*, *Sheila-Na-Gig*, and elsewhere. Her debut chapbook, *Escape and other poems*, was published by Kelsay Books in 2024. Currently she is reading for *The Adroit Journal*. Visit her at www.lesliehodgepoet.com.

The Twilight Years

Her voice is like the shawl that droops and falls

upon the floor, dust in tassels caught

while she walks and gestures as she drawls,

describing at great length the clothes she's bought.

She doesn't take a breath as she keeps talking.

Her eyes do not meet his except to see

that he is keeping pace, matching her walking

while paying close attention, and agrees.

Now in their twilight years, is this the best

that they can do? Is she too bored, too proud?

His morning coat, her satin wedding dress—

the seams unraveled, worn to shreds and shrouds.

"Forever wilt thou love, and she be fair"?

No. She doesn't know he doesn't care.

Lao Rubert lives in Durham, North Carolina. Her poems are forthcoming —or have appeared in *About Place Journal, Atlanta Review, Barzakh, Cider Press Review, Collateral, Pinesong Award Anthology, Poetry East, Rust & Moth, Spillway, The Avenue, The Marbled Sigh, Writers Resist* and elsewhere. Rubert holds an M.A. in English Literature from Duke University and has spent a career working to reform the criminal justice system.

Bereft

A ship of sadness sails each time she lifts

her dresser lid and presses rosehips to

her lips, reminder of her partner's gifts,

beloved fellowship she's come to rue.

The shipwreck of her heart is kept inside

her chest, a vessel filled with memories, left

within a packet sealed and long denied.

Survivorship remains. She's grown bereft.

What lengths her ladyship must go to keep

her cluttered shipyard closed and locked up tight

What hardships she must undergo to sleep,

to steer her armored battleship each night.

She orders breezy smiles throughout the day.

Her soul's midshipman halts, will not obey.

John Robinson is a mainstream, Appalachian-American poet and scholar from the Kanawha Valley in Mason County, West Virginia. His 182 literary works have appeared in 127 journals and presses throughout the United States, Australia, Canada, the United Kingdom, India, Poland, Germany and China. His first chapbook, *June's Fisher of Solitudes*, was published at Mountain State Press in March of 2025. He is also a published printmaker with 104 art images and photographs appearing in forty-two journals, electronic and print, in the United States, Italy, Ireland and the United Kingdom. Recent Literary Work; *Poet's Choice Anthology: Elegy, Ulu Review, Literary Yard, Language and Semiotic Studies, Origami Poets Project, Periodicities: A Journal of Poetry and Poetics, Mountain State Press, The Wallace Stevens Journal* and *Critical Survey*.

Keats

Because his name was writ in every breath.

He lived life's tidal gift, young bellows lung

filled with green joy, robust with so much heft.

Too soon, a thief took back the natural-hymn sung.

Pure life for living, set ablaze in pastoral spring,

no ego, politic pulpit or pew to groan

or sway in sleep.

    Thrust in awe these lines yet sing,

melodic psalm of truest leaf above the drone.

No fact or theory could ever shine or shimmer there as bright,

nor even burst forth as ever rushed a thirsting wind.

These eyes that sought which had true sight

this sacred thing beyond the cross, meekly of a thought rescind.

Why cling at all if fractured by burden, weary or lost?

Only for this love we hold, regardless of all cost.

Violet-May Davey is a creative, British author/poet with two short stories published by the Academy of Real Assets in 2022/2023. She also has 4 sonnet poems published in April 2025 and a short story in June 2025 by the Writer's Publishing Company. She loves reading for pleasure; writing many genres; drawing; learning new things; and going to museums and theatres. Currently taking a BA course in Creative Writing and English Literature at the University of Westminster.

Can Opposites Really Attract?

In many worlds with different people,

No one can ever truly be the same.

They all could be described as very sheeple,

Falling for a similar game.

Games of love that lead to doom,

With changes and a fatal heartbreak.

A whole life of inevitable gloom,

Slithering through opposite paths like a snake.

As the chaotic day turns into night,

Two destined lovers will secretly meet.

For if their relationship comes to light,

They will become apart and incomplete.

And although opposites can love,

Will face challenges not unheard of.

Estelle Tudor is an award-winning, multi-genre author from the land of myth and legend: Wales, where she lives with her husband, four children and dog writing muse. She is the author of 14 published novels, and has also been published in numerous anthologies and magazines too.

Fae Sonnet

Don't go in to the fairy ring at night

The trees warn me in the darkening wood

But I can't resist the glow of fae light

Never doing as Mama said I should

A piping song beckons sweetly to me

While tantalising scents tickle my nose

Never once did I think I ought to flee

As the toadstools caps gleam red like a rose

Come dance with us, a musical voice calls

And laughing, I cross over the threshold

But instantly the glittering light falls

My mind stolen, and my body left cold

So let that be a lesson to you, dears

Flee the fae ring or face your darkest fears

Leanne Moden is a writer, based in Nottingham. She's performed her poetry all over the UK and Europe, and was a semi-finalist at the BBC Edinburgh Fringe Slam in 2018. Her second pamphlet of poetry, _Get Over Yourself_, was published with Burning Eye Books in 2020. She's currently working on her first play.

Fen Vixen

She takes the idle viewer unawares

and sets the woods alight with memories.

Her spark ignites the grass, the thicket flares;

a flash of amber, darting through the trees.

Her tail, a plume of copper-coloured smoke,

the scent of burning catching on the breeze.

Her wistful longing grabs you by the throat

and smears your face with smouldering debris.

I've seen the vixen sleeping on the Fen

on land abandoned by retreating seas.

The sediment erupts. Her fiery den

a legacy that she destroys with ease.

Nostalgia is a creature built of flame;

You leave this place with nothing but your name.

Previously published on 28SonnetsLater.blogspot.com

Ecdysis

Tonight, I feel compelled to shed my skin

and hurl this tarnished outer self aside.

I ask you for relief and you provide.

You tranquillise me with your liar's grin.

A schism of the body and the mind—

like exorcising every anxious thought.

We can't always unlearn the things we're taught.

Tonight, I want to leave myself behind.

Another drink, and all the layers shift—

my outline fractures, leaves a perfect shell.

She looks just like me, eyes as dark as hell.

This hollow shadow woman is a gift.

Irresolute, her name dies in my throat;

the empty bottle makes the lowest note.

Previously published on 28SonnetsLater.blogspot.com

Creation With an Axe

A blazing, sanguinary wound of light,

this reddish star— our sun— a brutal breach.

The viscera of moonlight bleeds through night

and stains the sky with triumphs out of reach.

While shoulder blade tectonics move beneath

the sinew soil of slowly shifting dunes,

Creation swings its axe and grinds its teeth

and softly hums an ever-changing tune.

A god can give their body to the earth,

their bones transferred to sediment and scree.

A violent world demands a violent birth;

the axe must bite the bark to fell the tree.

A god can give their body to the earth;

a violent world demands a violent birth.

Previously published on 28SonnetsLater.blogspot.com. Republished in in Hecate Magazine (2021); republished in Seedlings Magazine (2024)

Rohan Buettel lives in Canberra, Australia. His haiku appear in Australian and international journals (including *Presence, Cattails* and *The Heron's Nest*). His longer poetry appears in various journals, including *Rattle, The Goodlife Review, Meanjin, Meniscus* and *Quadrant*.

The Dolphin

One morning drive, a lonely ocean way,

the blinding sun dazzling from monster swell,

I glancing saw a grey shape emerge through spray,

down precipitous slope tail thrusts propel

to quickly execute a bottom turn

and power up the face of the glassy wave,

then reach the crest and dive over the churn

to disappear into the roiling lave.

A dolphin surfs inside a mounting surge

with streamlined shape to minimise the drag,

slide through laminar planes, waters diverge.

Seen once, human surfers no longer brag.

Superb mastery, a dolphin at play,

being itself, the most perfect display.

Previously published in Quadrant

The Green Parasol

(After the painting by E. Phillips Fox)

The nineteenth century still lingers on

In summer 1912, a wicker chair

A Brisbane girl in Paris, c'est si bon

The filtered sunlight tints her auburn hair

And all is peaceful green, it bathes her face

Her hands, her skin, the trees, the garden bed

The creamy dress a shroud with verdant lace

The flowers white and pink and poppy red

She sits so calm, relaxed, untroubled there

Upon her lap she strokes her little dog

Her lustrous beauty shines through limpid air

A sunlit joy before the yellow fog

For few short years remain to live this way

Bloody carnage will blast this world away

Previously published in Quadrant

Gerburg Garmann, an accomplished painter and poet who, after a fulfilling tenure as a Professor of Global Languages and Cross-Cultural Studies at the University of Indianapolis, is now channeling her extensive cross-cultural insights into her art. With scholarly works published in English, German, and French, and a global presence in art and poetry anthologies, Gerburg brings a truly international perspective. She particularly focuses on creating meaningful art for women. Dive deeper into her creations at www.gerburggarmann.com.

Avian Vestiges

When birds shed wings, their skulls briefly part ways,

Evading full collapse, a bone's weak grace.

You've seen those silver beads in sunlit haze,

Where delicate wings once held their aerial space.

A testament to storms, a life once bold,

Now marked by absence, proof of tempests flown.

The horizon soon devours what's left untold,

Their scattered bones, to nature's depths are sown.

A day both cruel and innocent descends,

With languid greens and yellows soft and mild.

No rescue ships appear as daylight ends,

No mother's truths for young, with wisdom tiled.

So, blink and heed the signs, the fading light,

For other lives now claim the coming night.

The Golden Swarm

Now golden bugs, with tails of black and red,

Dart frenzied past the birds' forgotten dust.

Around you and your kin, their dance is spread,

A vibrant hum of life, a primal lust.

They weave through air where former wings once beat,

Ignoring every trace of what was lost.

No elegy for life's swift, grand defeat,

Just motion, purpose, at creation's cost.

Embracing every soul, these creatures fly,

In swallows quick, a tapestry unseen.

Threaded in fabric 'gainst the fading sky,

A new existence where the old has been.

No thought remains of those who graced the blue,

The golden swarm forgets, and carries through.

Twilight's Breath

They sway within twilight's gentle, whispered breath,

These tiny forms, their presence light and free.

The birds forgotten, claimed by time and death,

No memory remains for them to see.

And you too, in this vast, indifferent scheme,

Will fade and join the remnants of the past.

A fleeting thought, a momentary dream,

As nature's cycles endlessly hold fast.

The universe, in its majestic sweep,

Acknowledges no center, no grand claim.

It cradles life, then casts it in the deep,

A silent witness to a nameless game.

So, watch the bugs, their dance, their vibrant flight,

For you, like birds, will vanish into night.

Edward Heathman grew up in South Wales. He has had writing published in *The Manchester Review, The Manchester Anthology, The Visual-Verse Anthology, Poetry Wales*, the *Bluebird Anthology*, and on *Ink, Sweat & Tears*. He lives in Stockport, and in his spare time runs a YouTube channel, *Gagging4Lit*, where he talks about books.

California King Bed

Picturing Rihanna   stirred from her siesta,

bare feet pacing   the floor of   this rented place,

hair affectedly   tumbling over her shoulders   the colour

of the most lurid   most livid, wanting-attention   red,

her beautiful   hands gracing   the diaphanous curtains

that blow so gently in the soft-focussed   sea-ushered breeze,

on that   huge bed,   the sort of bed   I could sleep so richly on

it wouldn't matter even if you were here   with me,

because there's more than enough   space   for two,

and my dreams   would gather the slow   acoustic scrapes

of my longing   into an all-out   electric   guitar solo

the way a hurricane   forms   so harmlessly   over

the ocean,   rousing nature with it   as it goes,   agitating

any debris of what once was   us, those love-dyed memories.

Deborah Ketai (she/her) writes from the intersection of bipolarity, bisexuality, and creative self-doubt, leavened with humor and wordplay. Her work has appeared in *Think, Rattle*, and many other publications. She and her wife live in Connecticut's Naugatuck River Valley.

Chamber Music

What can I say to players long engaged

who finally stand ready to commit

to bring their music to this final stage

and join their melodies in perfect fit?

In chamber music, all must harmonize

and soloists their brilliancies submerge.

Though egos may recoil from compromise

and wish to dominate, resist the urge!

How shall you play when neither one must lead,

when tuning must be tempered, tempos kept

by no conductor save your hearts? You'll need

to know your parts, and further, to accept

the momentary dissonance of grace

notes. Drop the score: Just listen and embrace.

4 a.m.

Unbroken morning rolls in minutes slow

No birdsong yet, no headlights pierce the air

No paling of the dark, just silent time

and nothing in my heart to offer in prayer

The bed I left an hour ago has cooled

on my side, yours still giving way beneath

your weight. Your breath and dreams do not disturb

the mist, the still stale air surrounding me

No ghost reveals itself, no muse speaks low

and clear, no god invests my spirit now—

I am awake but still insensate to

the waiting world, I do not spark or glow

with amber thought, the fog does not abate

I only sit in solitude and wait

Valerie Little studied creative writing at Penn and Penn State University. Her creative non-fiction has twice been nominated for a Pushcart Prize. Her debut chapbook, *Little Blue Primer*, was a poetry finalist for the 16th Annual National Indie Excellence Awards. Valerie is a member of the Minnesota Orchestra and works in the funeral service industry.

Classify

You fox tied to a hollow, plastic chair.

Go drag it south to shirk apology.

And while she holds your sons, do you compare

our laughs and limbs, dark hair by perigee?

We creep towards middle age like primrose green.

Coy tartan, you're an empty set by choice.

Your tin man's algebra hides in between

your bird box smirk and mezcal nightshade voice.

You spilled loneliness across your blue tweed coat

and Scrabble made you hot last New Year's Eve.

Is an NDA abstention's antidote?

I'll sign for blithe affection's apogee.

You sloppy cocksure prince, your math's not right.

Lambert awaits, chrome darling, please don't miss your flight.

Mark Andrew Heathcote is an adult learning difficulties support worker. His poems have been published in journals, magazines, and anthologies online and in print. He is from Manchester and resides in the UK. Mark is the author of *In Perpetuity* and *Back on Earth*, two books of poems published by Creative Talents Unleashed.

Bleary-eyed beauty

Bleary-eyed beauty, of aromas sweet

By tinctures of air on the lilac leaf.

Give me not one broken remote heartbeat.

That's been crushed of all scents; it's self-belief.

Be not the pallor of unending grief.

Be the hedge rose in rosiness— discreet.

A warm little dear, where all bees compete

Garden me a blush beneath your kerchief.

So that I might be your one knight's motif:

I'll draw a glance that others meet defeat.

Yours is the world above and below my feet.

The moon climbs on aural wings— stays too brief.

Such is the allure of the stars in Orbit.

My soul's heart, yours, spoken in a sonnet?

Vaishnavi Pusapati is a poet previously published in *Roanoke Review, Prole, Inkpantry, Bare Hill Review, Heron's Nest,* among others.

Of Light and Dark

Remember, as a child, I feared the dark,

Yet now I'm frightened by the glare of light;

I sit alone and watch one distant spark,

A bed-lamp burning through another's night.

Perhaps they pace, or ponder while they weep,

Or cry into the pillows they have known;

The moon and I keep silver watch as sleep

Falls on the street, yet stirs with undertone.

The street cats dream with cheeks on folded paws,

While grief's young saplings rise to block the sun;

The pills take root, enforcing quiet laws,

Till all my battles seem already done.

And light or dark, both shadow me the same,

Till night alone permits my grief to name.

Betwixt Dreams and Daylight

Betwixt the dream and day my soul abides,

Where shadows bloom and breathe the truest light;

The waking world, a pause where joy subsides,

A fleeting shore that yields to endless night.

I build my hopes like castles near the tide,

Each wave a hand to tear their towers down;

Yet still I guard them, though they turn and hide,

Like wayward children straying from the town.

If dreams were flesh, they'd walk to school by now,

And I would tell them what they mean each day;

But paper dolls dissolve, and I allow

Their fragile forms to drift and fade away.

Yet time, like distance, may my loss restore,

And grant me dawn where dark shall fall no more.

David Ram's sonnets appear in numerous magazines and anthologies, including *Amethyst Review, Gargoyle Online, Meat for Tea: Valley Voices, Sport Literate, The Orchards Poetry Journal*, and elsewhere. He retired from teaching community college and lives with his wife in western Massachusetts, where he practices writing, rowing and grandparenting.

Broad Brook Basin

My dory drifts a shallow filled with clouds

and trees. No sights or sounds of hawks or crows

as now the brood of geese has gone for good.

A playful flight of visiting swallows

converts this cove into a water park.

Performing acrobatic dips and climbs,

the families circle in cheerful arcs

attached to invisible pendulums.

They glide above the surface or even

skim the surface, shaking dry of droplets

by surging in and out of shade and sun.

In what resonate like rhyming couplets,

they chatter, sing and murmur, all and each,

a liquid language far beyond my reach.

Previously published in The Orchards Poetry Journal: 145 (Summer 2025)

Hockey Jersey 18

Should I compare you to your father's day?

You are more lively and more talented,

and all who watch remark, *That girl can play*.

The moves you make can't be defended:

the curl and drag or deke and dangle,

a cross-ice saucer to thread the needle,

or one-touch pass to feed a triangle.

Whether down the boards or up the middle

you handle pucks with poise. On the backcheck

you give it all you've got. Feet moving, stick

on stick you angle 'em off, strongly poke

the puck away appearing very slick.

    You skate within yourself till a linesman

    whistles then curse out loud, *Too many men*.

Previously published in Sport Literate: Autumnal Road, 15.2: 109 (Fall 2023)

Public Skating

In too loose laces and all alone you

set your skates upon the indoor ice, slip

and slide as if an otter in the zoo.

You begged off the frozen pond to trip

around the rink where big kids play, to step

inside the team benches and through the glass

then travel all around the giant loop

along the boards, letting nobody pass,

beyond the red cage, behind the goal line

and then, best of all, the Zamboni door,

and, oh, careful now, sneak past the sin bin

where the zebra sends you if you play poor.

You shuffle once around the arena,

laughing to yourself like a hyena.

Previously published in Grand Little Things online (2/12/23)

Ben Goldnagl is a queer London-based poet and costume maker originally from Austria. He has been previously published in *Stepaway Magazine*.

Note:

Ben long loved Shakespeare's sonnets and have thought of them as a kind of encyclopedia of love matters. One element of love that he doesn't speak to at length, however, is self-love, especially in hard times, which they have attempted to cover in this poem.

Appendix C

How could I have been made to hold an ocean

And to have room in me for all its might

And still be nauseated by its motion

A harboured body tossed from side to side

I'd rather be a ship at sea for weeks

That too would be a rough and wretched ride

But while I tumble over crashing peaks

My hull would know to keep the sea outside

But space is what an ocean truly needs

Give in and open up your hatches wide

Then you can soften as your sea recedes

And rage in rhythm with your rising tide

You are the vessel that contains the sea

And you must let it move you endlessly.

Joshua Walker is a poet whose work blends classical forms with contemporary themes. His poetry explores the complexities of human emotion and experience, drawing inspiration from both traditional and modern sources. Joshua's work has been featured in various literary journals and anthologies, and he is committed to the craft of poetry

For Love, I Laid My Sword Beside the Flame

I bore the crest of kings upon my shield,

And swore no heart should rule me but the crown—

Yet when her eyes undid what war had sealed,

I let the empire in my veins fall down.

My oaths were carved in marble, cold and bright,

But softer arms drew fire from frozen stone.

Her kiss made mockery of armored might,

And I betrayed the throne to be alone.

Let history forget my name in shame,

Let songs be sung of braver men than I—

For what is glory but a fleeting flame

That leaves the soul to smolder when it dies?

I chose her breath above the breath of kings,

And now I wear a crown of lesser things.

Lynn D. Gilbert's poems, twice nominated for Pushcart Prizes, have appeared in such journals as *Appalachian Review, Arboreal, Blue Unicorn, carte blanche, Light, The MacGuffin, and Sheepshead Review*. A founding editor of *Borderlands: Texas Poetry Review*, she lives in an Austin suburb and reviews poetry submissions for *Third Wednesday* journal.

Cassandra's Complaint

Apollo, I see what no one wants to hear:

People arrive at death in moral shock

not knowing why they lived or who they were;

our species runs to dash itself on rocks;

the millions starve for no more worthy cause

than others' whim, greed, vengeance, will to power,

indifference, urge to vindicate the laws

of Marx or market, theory of the hour.

Justice does happen, yes! It gropes by chance

through winding corridors to a bored court

where litigants will spend their years in a trance

of hatred, stays, and motions— deadly sport.

Can I, or any, cut this monstrous waste?

—*With sight and speech, not action, were you graced.*

Previously published in The Decadent Review

Vanessa Caraveo is an award-winning author, published poet, and artist whose literary work brings focus to various social issues that exist today. She has been published in *Literature Today Journal, The Poet Magazine, Latinidad Magazine, Poetrybay, Anacua Literary Arts Journal*, and in multiple anthologies throughout the years.

The Sun's Goodbyes

When daylight seeks its humble place to rest,

the golden sun will lay his head down low,

as if to kiss the earth from distant west,

to paint the skies in fire's light amber glow.

The clouds that often offer ample shade

become backdrops of yellow, orange, and red.

The shadows stretch their limbs where space is made,

and each small ounce of light is spent and bled.

A promise to return with morning's light

as ends another fleeting dreamlike day.

Old sun goes down and softly out of sight.

So ends all time for work and kiddish play.

Perhaps to grant a moment wreathed in peace,

the sun descends and all things slowly cease.

A Seashore Sonnet

Upon a shore where waves all go to play,

the Ocean sighs, her voice so soft and sweet.

The golden sands embrace the tide's delay,

as seagulls dance on tender, flighty feet.

A breeze, as if to tickle yonder cheek

ignites the air with salt and wind combined.

And distant sails glide hereabouts to seek

a humble port, of tight and strict design.

Here time itself is lulled to soft repose,

beside the subtle sights and scents of sea.

A place where kelp and stillness surely grow,

the border of all things born truly free.

Souls linger here, where Ocean sings her song.

The home of life, to which we all belong.

Najka Altazy has been an archivist and librarian for the last fifteen years at the National Archives, the Smithsonian, and the Folger Shakespeare Library. He has published more than a hundred theater reviews and has produced bar Shakespeare and interactive performance art. He lives in Alexandria, VA with a lady, a girl, and a boy, only one of whom is a dog.

Jam Session

[To BAK, dated 7/27/2025]

Our season-long tradition traps the sunlight

Where sticky fingers cup the juicy rain.

We pucker at the acid's needed bite

That forms a plasma out of sugar cane.

There was a time when "helping" slowed me down;

The dog would hover at your splattered feet,

But now your knife's your own. We both are proud,

For children ripen faster than a peach.

Your skin will thicken through the sucrose steam.

Your hand will leopard with a spray of scars.

As painful as your scalded tongue may seem,

It won't outlast this summer in a jar.

We harvest fruit the farmer left, refused,

And know the flesh is sweeter for the bruise.

Erica Berquist has worked as a freelance editor and for Cloudmed Solutions LLC as a Recovery Analyst since graduating from Towson University with a BS in English,. Her poetry, non-fiction works, and short stories have been published in numerous literary magazines, blogs, and anthologies. One of her short story publications "Coffin Bell" won second place in Commuter Lit's Halloween Week 2024 Contest, and her poem "Ulmus" was a top finalist in Wingless Dreamer's Roots and Rivers Poetry Contest. Erica's debut novel, _The Servant_, was published by Poets Choice & Free Spirit LLC in April 2025. In her free time, she enjoy making jewelry, researching family history for herself and others, gardening, and spending time with cats.

Photinus macdermotti

Come, take my hand my dear, as spring is here.

The first fireflies are out, let's go down

By the big lake where you can hold me near

As the bright fireflies spark around us now.

When summer air rests heavily on us,

You press your lips against mine and make vows.

We lay beside our lake, entwined at dusk,

As the bright fireflies court around us now.

As autumn leaves drift across the old lake,

The lips I once kissed now twist with a scowl.

And I have to ask you, was it all fake?

As the bright fireflies fade around us now.

People say that fireflies will all be gone soon,

Yet I will always think about that June.

Caidan Walker is a poet studying English Literature and Creative Writing at Cornell University. He is the 1st Place Prize recipient of the George Harmon Coxe Poetry Award, as well as the Editor-in-Chief and founder of *Lucky Lizard Journal*. He has one chapbook titled *Vale* (Kelsay Books, 2024) and his poetry appears in various journals and magazines, including *The Round, Home Planet News,* and *Third Wednesday*. His website is www.cwalkerpoetry.com.

The Coin of Apocalypse

His hand conducts the opus of all things;

What majesty holds He! Like ancient love,

That richness holds us taut and, bursting, sings

In voice that raised the Heavens up above.

My Father holds a coin within that hand

With sin upon the back, and on the face

A Son with fine brass foot that walked this land

And eyes aflame with destiny and grace,

His hair a white like wool or fallen snow

And garment girt with girdle gleaning gold,

A water-lamming voice that seems to know

That we His paltry people shan't be sold,

But free we walk, and so he flips the coin

And waits to see which children shall rejoin.

Heidi Joffe(M.Ed. MFA) is a poet and multimedia artist who crafts with fibers, clay, and words. She writes essays and screenplays, but poetry is her sustenance. Her publication homes include *Panoply, The Opiate, Sheila-Na-Gig, Gyroscope, Pine Mountain Sand and Gravel,* and Hercules Press. She received her MFA from Pacific University.

Old World Cuckoo

I capture rainwater in broken bowls;

in trees, I hear birds nest for their eggs,

but also a cuckoo calls, not without soul

in its treachery, plumage and twig legs

deliver eggs to a surrogate to love

these intruders, nurture them with pain

of doting. With tumult of eagle above

all I can do is plant my seeds and wait.

This pied-eyed bird flew across continents

to land on this cedar's shaggy limbs.

Perhaps like me, it had to learn to mend

by leaving home, far from familiar dins,

distorted, torqued, a wing that bends

towards Desolation Sound on wind and whim.

Numerology of 14

Ok, little song, let's hear it on point, in form

from five stresses per line and the pause

between thoughts, or phrase. Cease whining.

Is a poem a game, or something more full

filled with mind afoot, and love in a frown.

We speak today of a past and future curled

into our dna, spirals that begin to shape me,

that return to a space from a different place,

angled so acutely that it intrudes and distorts

my time and space, all continuum feels cast adrift,

offbeat, uneven, scattered beads of metal liquids,

And I, with crystal bowls and sound healings, body

in turmoil, regret that grounds in nothing, yes no

thing bleeds enough to hold my thinning blood.

On Assassins

(for Coleman and Hayes)

a waxing gibbous moon peers between the firs,

her profile glows at me or glowers at my bad

attitude, my leg on table, my ashtray half

filled. I'm supposed to think about sonnets,

but the moon gathers my thoughts, the twisted

bits, caught on psalms and amens, ancient strings

strummed under this moon,watching all,

spy on prophecy and pyres, nuptial to grave,

and my dog, who snores, bored with this story,

her tides turn towards my pillow, to dreams of dirt,

grass, maybe the neighbor's cat in her grasp,

not to the sky. or a book on the table— it holds

me prisoner, caught in blush inducing memory,

oh, moon, how to assess the damage I wrought.

Rajeshwar Prasad, born in Bela, Aurangabad, Bihar, India, on 26 August 1970, the pioneer of the Theatre of the Absurd in India, is a poet, playwright, novelist, essayist, researcher, philosopher, thinker and academician. He is a prominent figure in English literature who infuses meaningful philosophical insights into appealing stories. With a Ph.D. exploring Christopher Marlowe's lyricism and many years of service as a Professor, he draws on the strengths of both worlds. He is the author of many thought-provoking plays, including *The Travellers, The Wife, The Tribute, Zero into Four, Teachers' Day, Zero into Nine,* and *Zero into Plus;* the insightful fiction, *"Righteousness"*; and collections of powerful poetry, including *Gandhi— the Messiah* and *Bullet Land*, all published by TSL Publications, Rickmansworth, UK. His epic, *The Gandhi-Gita*, the novels, *Dance of Democracy*, *Now, Forever Yours,* and the reflective essays in *Hello Life* show the author's scope. His life of teaching and creative writing demonstrates his commitment to enhancing mind and soul. He has been honoured with several national and international awards in Literature and Education. He has also published 26 research articles, along with 9 essays, short stories and poems, published in the reputed journal *The Aerial Perspective*, Quillkeepers Press, LLC, US, and some other international journals.

He was honoured with the 'Asian Excellence Award 2024' for the 'Best Professor of the Year', the 'Award of Excellence' for the 'Indian Icon Educational Entrepreneur', 2 times 'Golden Book Awards' for his books *Zero Into Four* and *Dance of Democracy*, 2 times 'Sahitya Sparsh Awards' for his books *The Travellers* and *Gandhi— the Messiah* 'Top 10 Rising Leaders Awards', 'Top 100 leaders Awards', Ukiyoto Literary Awards for his book entitled *Righteousness*, Visionary Indians Award 2025 and 'National Teacher of the Year Award 2025'.

Screen Shadows

Alas, the bright screen, a splashing stage,

Entices away from green, sunny meads,

To rushing rivers, and a fleet'ng image,

And cracked thoughts, providing fragile needs.

A clock to tick, not a stop, countless times,

Each second split, a sweet, eager will,

We chase the pace and run against primes,

And find our souls, e'er a bittersweet pill.

Not only pleasure, but also a mess,

Where echo'ng place of the virtual world,

A heart is too humane, even distance,

A hidden mean'ng of this assured land.

Yet hope exists, flashes in each soul,

To acquire our way, and set us close whole.

LaVern Spencer McCarthy, a Texas native, has published five books of poetry and four books of short stories. Her poems have been published in *Visions International, Poetry Society of Texas Book of The Year, Open Skies Quarterly, National Federation of State Poetry Society's Encore, Austin Poetry Society's Austin's Best Poets, A Texas Garden of Verses* as well as numerous state anthologies and newspaper columns. She, is a life member of Poetry Society of Texas. She has published five books of poetry, six books of short stories, and three journals. She has won over five-hundred state awards and forty-one national awards

In This Land

Had freedom never been reality

for me, I might be happy as a slave,

in love with every shackle binding me

in innocence, from childhood to the grave.

Sustained with love of liberty, I share

endeavors for a better life. My goal?

I never shall succumb to hatred's snare,

or wear the tarnish of a traitor's soul.

In foreign places tyranny is king.

Dictators wield their swords and never sleep.

Imprisoned subjects there can only sing

their broken songs of misery. I weep

for those whose chains will never let them fly,

for I am blessed with wings that touch the sky.

Frank J. Albert lives in Western Pennsylvania and has taught Humanities courses in several Pittsburgh area colleges. His work has appeared in literary journals including *Cedar Rock, Orchards Poetry Journal, Armstrong Literary,* and *Literary Heist*. Please visit his Facebook page Frank J. Albert, Author.

What to Make of Time

A rosebud blooms, a leaf grows red in turn;

a loss, a gain, another season new.

The give and take of time is what we learn

when we recall our days of passion true.

But what can we as lovers hope to gain

by dwelling on a time before we came

together seeking shelter from the rain

that drowns a heart and clouds each day the same?

My love, *our* time began one summer day

when first we kissed and wiped away the past,

so, like two architects we sketch the way

to build a life and love we know will last.

Like mythic lovers who deserve their fame,

let us renew our passion's faithful flame.

Janice Katz is the Coordinator of Pediatric Education at Fort Bragg in North Carolina. She is passionate about the humanities and poetry and incorporates this passion into her teaching. She is one of the original founders of the William Carlos Williams poetry competition for medical students. Her work has been presented orally at Humanities and Medicine conferences across the country and has been contributed to an anthology at Eckerd College.

Perpetual Eclipse

There is a space between the night and day

which hovers neither black nor with new light

but holds approaching morning soft at bay

and presses upon dreams. Such is its might.

To stall the creep of time, to integrate

the ground with sky. To stretch the owling hoot,

prohibiting the muses to abate.

and giving joy a place to plant its root.

So prance between the eve and sleeping morn.

Uncover revel, find clandestine fete.

Abandon obligations, feel newborn,

without intent. Rawboned. Inviolate.

When such eclipse forbids the dawning light

There is no end to celebrated night.

Aims and Ends

Like most intentions yours possessed a spark

of promise, said 'forever' with one breath.

Provided paint to saturate the stark

dry canvas which had come before. Made death

of former ways. Seducer with a charm,

creating darkly beautiful vignettes,

your story-telling able to disarm

suspicion. Nimbly hedging every bet.

But weakness hovered there along your brow

pervading even wink and winning smile.

Questioning whether you'd survive, and how

when darkness pressed or terror stayed awhile.

Despite beguiling promises and song

The longest race is only for the strong.

R.J. Breathnach (he/him/sé/é) is an award-winning Irish writer, Wexford-born and Meath-based. His work has been published in *ROPES Literary Journal, The Wexford Bohemian,* and *The Honest Ulsterman*, among others. His debut poetry chapbook, *I Grew Tired of Being a Zombie*, was published by Alien Buddha Press in 2021.

A Sonnet on Betrayal

Betrayal is the gravest sort of sin.

Dante's final inferno deems it so.

Thus when we feel it burn beneath our skin

Deep down though hell's dark circles we must go.

To see the fate awaiting those who prey

Upon the unworldly, the outstretched hand.

They who take a friendship and then one day

Cast you, their friend, unto the desert sand.

Comradery, a fickle thing is not.

Illusions of it burn away like coals

Upon the flames, the circles burning hot,

Where Lucifer will chew upon their souls.

A traitor is the lowest form of life.

Each breath they take, another cause for strife.

A.C. Blake is a Canadian-American author and illustrator whose poetry, stories, and art are shaped by her roots and a deep love of cultural history. Her award-winning work-blending humor, insight, and emotional resonance— has been published and exhibited internationally. A retired professor of visual storytelling, she continues to create work rooted in what matters most to her: nature, memory, and meaning. Her recent poetry book, *Celebrating Maud: A Tribute to L.M. Montgomery*, received the International Impact Award for Poetry. Her work appears in anthologies such as *Remembering Sylvia Plath, Walt Whitman 205*, and the forthcoming collection *In the Weeds: A Field Guide for the Tangled Seasons*. To learn more, visit annecatharineblake.com.

The Reader Who Stays

They do not rush or force the tale to start,

But enter gently— eyes like turning leaves.

They read not just the words but feel the heart,

And linger where the margin softly grieves.

They trace the silence folded in my lines,

And call it beautiful instead of weak.

They turn the pages others leave behind,

And never flinch when plot or shadow speaks.

They hold the book with reverence, not pride,

Returning not for ending, but for soul.

No need to solve or tuck my truths inside—

They love the ache, the dreamscape, and the whole.

I am no task, no treasure to possess—

Just story, loved with presence, not redress.

Subhashree is from Odish, India. She is currently pursuing her Master's in English and Comparative Literature from Pondicherry University. A feminist, a cinephile, a reader. She has previously been published on various digital platforms, including *Orange Peel, Xinsai, Catheartic, Ink and Marrow.*

A Sonnet for My City

My city of birth, my city of love

Looks more romantic now in days and nights

As I soar towards a new dream, to rove

Seeing sadness dangle in the grand lights.

Evenings mumble through softness of pink grief

For me to catch the light breeze of memories

Secrets stored in skyscrapers play mischief

The roads turn to write forgotten stories.

But a new city calls me, dreams await

For me to fall in love, begin again

So, I mourn for the remembrance of late

As I prepare for goodbyes, all in vain.

I will someday cry for my city's name

I will come back with my passion of fame.

Ellen Harrold (She/Her) is an Irish artist, writer and editor-in-chief of *Metachrosis Literary*. She uses painting, drawing, text, and textiles to explore anatomy and physics through creative abstraction. She has exhibited her art with the Irish Museum of Modern Art (*Earth Rising*, 2024), Lido Stores Margate (*If Heaven Falls*, 2025), and An Stiúideo Kerry (*Soilsiú*, 2025). She has also recently published art in *The Storms, An Áitiúil,* and *Orion*. She has published poetry in English and Irish in magazines such as *Shearsman, The Pomegranate*, and *Channel*. She has a website: ellenharrold.art, an Instagram: @ellenharroldart, and a Bluesky: @ellenharrold

Streetlight

Above, dusk collapses in misshapen shrines.

Drowning in pale blues and heavy umber,

the patterns of brushwood roads, serpentine.

Abloom briny eaves, stone facade slumber.

Submerged to overtures, fluorescent din

congeals eventide hues to murky lead.

Closed eyes bely impurity. My skin,

luscent, hides starlight. Pollution dispread.

Sorrel, sheep's-bit, and gorse arise the verge,

gently undo these coarse supports. Release

unearthly murmurations. Demiurge

consign my hapless yearning, render peace

to canthus aches behind my eyes. Recall

opaque descents to frail curtain call.

Logan McDermott-Mostowy is an educator and librarian from

Washington, DC. You can find their work in DC-based literary mag *Lilac Peril.*

perennial
(sonnet for a spring morning)

in empty verse I dreamed all winter through

as cold sun painted silver on my cheeks.

and in the half-light all I saw was you,

a demiurge, the heir of ardent greeks.

I cast my hope in marble, lest it rot;

called you an idle shadow in the cave.

but in my eager worship I forgot

that flowers, more than granite, mend a grave.

let cities fall and statues start to crack—

a truer beauty blooms in softer hues.

let earth reclaim the scars that line her back—

if growth is chaos, this is one I choose.

though once I blossomed lonely in the night,

as love is change, I open to your light.

Sally Mills graduated as an artist and followed a career devoted to nature conservation, she has written/illustrated three publications: her debut memoir, <u>Island to Island</u>, and accompanying Photograph Collection, together with the production of illustrations for a children's book, Boomy the Bittern. With drive and motivation to inspire people about nature, she has recently become captivated by the world of poetry. She has had children's poems published by the Dirigible Balloon and has recently had poems selected by *The Toy and Little Thought Press* magazines. Her poetry for adults is due to appear in two anthologies.

The Observer

The natural world has always been my thing,

I watch and listen, try to understand

the autumn migrants, arrivals in spring,

the choices they make and their master plan,

what they need to exist. But how it's changed,

the rollcall at dawn appears lesser now,

birds leave, don't return as if they're estranged,

the swifts and nightingales are silent, that's how

we tell it's different we spot the signs,

the heat, the christened storms, the flooded plains,

what scientists find too hard to define,

the pesky verbal threats of climate change.

We're not immune, I ponder what it means,

ashamed, I wipe my binoculars clean.

Shreya is a Dubliner, poet and neurodivergent woman. Originally from India, she has now called Ireland home for five years. She works in tech by day and stretches her evenings and weekends in books and Word docs. She is among the ten emerging English language poets to be selected for Poetry Ireland Introductions 2025. She was the featured artist in online journal, *Tintreach*'s July issue and chosen to be a Voice of Peace Artist for Irish Peace and Human Rights festival 2025. She is currently representing Dublin in a UNESCO City of Literature writing exchange programme with Melbourne.

Sonnet 401(k):
The Cost of Living

It starts at a thousand euros per head

for spaces shared without utility,

food and water. But that's before you add

the fare and flair of clothes, mobility

and entertainment tax. Night outs are out

of scope. Sustainability's the rizz—

unless you are so lavishly burnt-out,

you see ten quid a pint and say, yes please!

Your bosses vest in millions' worth of stock

to stock mansions for which they've settled.

So what if it costs a thousand jobs in work-

force? Food and fuel supplies are throttled

while arms cross borders. The cost of living

is proportional to the cost of killing.

Previously published in Tintreach, the Smashing Times Arts & Literary Journal

Susan Irvine teaches a course on using smell as material at the Royal College of Art, London. She has published a novel, <u>Muse</u>, and a short story collection, *Corpus*, both with Quercus.

Snatch Fire

Snatch fire from heaven, what do you expect?

That God would be content to send a shower

Of rain to douse the flames and not resect

The offender from his sight? His mastering power

—You well know Eve— demands dominion,

Counts every ripening apple in his grove

And from his law grants no-one a secession—

Thou shalt not! Above all, thou shalt not have

The fire of love that's for the Gods alone

In their celestial pleasuring-ground above.

Prometheus taught us first the recursive pain

Of heavenly retribution; true love gone

Each night your broken heart heals up its hurt

Each morning finds its ragged rip retorn.

I loved you

I loved you. And when asked I shrug and say,

'The love that fed my life has lost its flame.

It's over. I've moved on. What's left is ash,

Weightless and grey discarded ghosts of pain.'

They nod, 'it's for the best, you've let him go,

At last. There's room now for new love to enter in.'

And they go home— good friends— and I to mine

And close the door on all that's past and done.

But when I lie alone, my mind unswept,

A shovelful of ashes for a heart,

And poke the slag that I should leave alone

I find that at the centre it's still red.

And then I know this love will never pass

But burn till I am ashes at the last.

Paul Burgess, an emerging poet, is the sole proprietor of a business in Lexington, Kentucky that offers ESL classes in addition to English, Japanese, and Spanish-language translation and interpretation services. He has recently contributed work to *Blue Unicorn, Light, The Orchards, Snakeskin, The Ekphrastic Review, The Asses of Parnassus,* and several other publications. https://paulburgesswritingandlanguage.blog/

The Darkling Thrush's Ear

You sense a change in winter's deathly hush.

A voice appears to warm the frozen gloom—

The vibrant song of Hardy's darkling thrush,

Perhaps an antidote to thoughts of doom.

I'd also love to hear that hopeful song

And don't intend to damage or destroy.

The awe I feel is just as deep and strong,

But what I hear aren't hymns of boundless joy.

I hear impassioned cries of pain and lust—

The songs of creatures singing just to cope,

Of birds that belt their tunes because they must

And sing of food and sex but never hope.

The darkling thrush's song may hold less cheer

For those who listen with a thrush's ear.

First published in The Orchards, Winter 2024

Elaine Desmond's poetry has appeared in *Hold Open the Door (Irish Chair of Poetry Anthology), The Ogham Stone, Hive Poetry Journal, Cork Words, Flora/Fauna Nature Anthology, Poetry in the Park,* and others. Commended / listed in the U.K. Poetry Society Competition, Allingham Festival, Gregory O'Donoghue, Frontier Roots & Roads, Letter Review, Westival, Winchester, Rialto Nature & Place, Mslexia Pamphlet and Fish Poetry Prizes. Elaine received an M.A. in Creative Writing and a Munster Literary Centre mentorship with poet Grace Wells. She is from near Skibbereen in Ireland.

Golden

Let me let you say you love me without

interruption, space to land your words, display

your raw heart. Let me stand there and take it not

flinching. Let me cup your hair-bun like a rare sea

urchin. Let me gunwale-lean with you to Sherkin.

Let me instead ask about your miscarriage.

Let me light Carroll after Carroll

for you. Let me take you out for coffee.

Let me let you wait by my bus stop, let

me not ask you to leave. Let us not fail

to embrace. Let me listen to say more.

Let me once reverence your bones alive,

hold them. Let me let you say whatever

you want but first let me say you were golden.

Damaris West studied French and Spanish at Oxford University before becoming a librarian, a tutor, and then a commercial writer. She currently lives in south-west Scotland, close to the sea. Her poetry has appeared widely in publications such as *Snakeskin, The Lake, Blue Unicorn, Allegro, Ink Sweat & Tears, Acumen, Gyroscope Review*, and *The Friday Poem*, and has been placed in several competitions, national and international. She is currently preparing a first collection under the auspices of Yaffle Press. She enjoys writing both free and formal verse. https://damariswest.site123.me

Penumbra

I lift my eyes to mountains, or to hills,

depending on translation of the word

from Hebrew though, except where custom wills,

the boundary between the two is blurred.

You cannot trace a margin in the sea

between a ripple and a shaft of light,

or read the writing of the wind on tree

and field, or pinpoint dusk becoming night.

No lines exist inside a mess of cloud,

no verge or pavement where the milky way

meanders foggy-footed through a crowd

of bluebells and an avenue of may.

Our lives are spent divided by a breath,

a veil, a membrane, from the black of death.

Beth Kanell lives in northeastern Vermont among rivers, rocks, and a lot of writers. Her poems seek comfortable seats in small, well-lit places, including *Lilith Magazine*, *The Comstock Review*, *Indianapolis Review*, *Gyroscope Review*, *The Post-Grad Journal*, *Does It Have Pockets?*, *Anti-Heroin Chic*, *Ritualwell*, *Persimmon Tree*, *Northwind Treasury*, *RockPaperPoem*, and *Rise Up Review*. Her collection *Thresholds* is due in early 2026 from Kelsay Books.

Visiting the House of Robert Frost— and His Wife Elinor

For twenty years I've climbed your homely hill.

This time the brook's wide crossing's been replaced

and someone's cut the shrubs— no berries fill

my eager hands. Such neatness; such a waste!

I see the dooryard's stayed about the same:

long-stemmed and bold, the sunset lilies rise,

surround the porch. But I've returned to blame

your landscape love, your lust for readers' eyes.

I know you better now, despite the room

where beeswaxed care maintains your desk, your chair.

I bite my tongue, my lips, I hiss and fume

for wife ignored and left outside your care.

How could I once have thought you wrote with grace

When not one poem of yours admires her face?

Yankee Girl

Her chestnut curls shone copper in the sun

and in the photo (lost!) so did her pride—

New England born and bred, she learned to ride

almost before her chubby legs could run.

This is the prize I think my father found:

new immigrant, he hungered to fit in,

draw to her certainty, her Yankee grin.

She teased him, boasting Revolution's ground.

Then, when his British soul clung to her voice

she wrapped him in her love, taught him to sing

the wild frontier, the country life! Her ring

in ruby, not in diamond, showed her choice.

Drawn to the new and bright, she loved their life

Until betrayal made her *'just his wife'*.

About Us

Quillkeepers Press, LLC is a small indie press and indie author resource group. We publish themed anthologies on a variety of topics, as well as provide resources and services to indie authors. We pride ourselves on the quality of our traditionally published titles, as well as our reasonably priced services for indie authors who prefer to do it themselves. It is a deep passion of ours to help as many writers' voices as possible be heard. As indie artists ourselves, we understand most creatives operate within a strict budget. Therefore, it has always been a priority of ours to keep our rates reasonable. Our corporate climate is not one of profit but one of helping bring dreams to fruition. Our motto sums it up best: *"Reading between the lines, to make your words take flight"*.

We produce between 3 and 6 anthologies annually. We don't charge artists to be published in our anthologies, although tips are welcome through Submittable.com to cover the cost of the ad space, ISBN number registration, copyright fees, as well as other overhead costs.

As writers ourselves, we understand how challenging the market can be and how difficult it is to get work into the hands of a larger audience. Therefore, we accept and encourage our contributors to submit both new and previously published compositions (as long as the previous publisher allows it). Too often, we find publishers who want exclusive rights to the work being published. This is counterproductive if the artist wants their message to reach as many people as possible. Having been in and studied the industry for years, our founder has concluded that many writers take great pride in their work and produce it for their own healing.

Furthermore, they share said work, hoping it helps others heal. For all the aforementioned reasons, it is our current policy to request non-exclusive rights to our contributors' work rather than exclusive rights. In essence, our artists are allowing us to borrow their prized writing, and we are incredibly grateful.

It is also for those same reasons that we consider ourselves an indie publishing services company, rather than a traditional publisher. Traditional publishing typically involves a lengthy contract, exclusive rights to work, and royalties. We would rather help wrap artists' products into a beautiful package and allow them to set their own parameters, price points, and keep all their royalties from sales.

On a final note, whether you have employed our services or lent us your voice in an anthology, thank you for entrusting us with your craft. If you would like to participate in a forthcoming anthology, please check out our Submittable page at www.submittable.com. For more information on our services, please visit our website www.quillkeeperspress.com

Keep the quill moving,

Stephanie Lamb, Founder, EIC

Quillkeepers Press, LLC

Other Books Produced by Quillkeepers Press

Soon, A New Day

A rise of the Phoenix-themed anthology of essays, memoirs, short stories, and poetry by various artist

Turning Dark into Light and Other Magic Tricks of the Mind

A mental health-themed anthology of essays, memoirs, short stories, and poetry by various artists

Rearing in the Rearview

A parenting-themed anthology of essays, memoirs, short stories, and poetry by various artists

Verbal Vomit and Other Poetry and Prose

A poetry and prose collection by Stephanie Lamb

Tan Lines

A Summer Solstice-inspired anthology of memoirs, short stories, and poetry by various artists.

Bare Bones

A Halloween-inspired anthology of essays, memoirs, short stories, and poetry by various artists.

Snowdrifts

A Winter Solstice-inspired anthology of essays, memoirs, short stories, and poetry by various artists.

Sapling

A Spring equinox-inspired anthology of essays, memoirs, short stories, and poetry by various artists.

Dislocated

The debut poetry collection by Dylan Webster.

Botany of Gaia

A nature-inspired anthology of essays, memoirs, short stories, and poetry by various artists.

Harvest

A Fall equinox-inspired anthology of essays, memoirs, short stories, and poetry by various artists.

The Matador's Wife

A chapbook-length collection of poetry by Andrés Colón.

scars & lyres

A chapbook-length collection of poetry by ww harris.

Inspired

An art-inspired-by-art anthology of essays, memoirs, short stories, poetry, and artwork.

Smitten

A love-inspired anthology of essays, memoirs, short stories, and poetry.

High Water

A chapbook-length collection of poetry by Carrie Carter.

Notable Moons

A Chapbook-length collection of poetry by David Gunton.

My West

A chapbook-length collection of poetry by Jenifer Fox.

Lightwaves

A YA Historical Fiction novella

AmerAsian

A poetry collection by Kimberly McAfee.

The Savior and the Shadow Queen

A poetry collection by Kimberly McAfee.

Turning the Corner

A poetry collection by Lori Ulrich.

Purge & Bloom

A chapbook-length poetry collection by Brooks Decker.

Arranging Words

A chapbook-length poetry collection by Fran Abrams.

Words for Women

A chapbook-length poetry collection by Lori Heninger.

Lent Words

A chapbook-length poetry collection by Christine Moore.

Talking to Ghosts

A chapbook-length poetry collection by Jon Tobias.

A House with Bad Bones

A poetry collection by Adeline Tatum

The Wake of the Hound Dogs

A witty must-read novel by AD Matson

Alchemies, Arrivals

An eco-poetry chapbook collection by Sophia Pinto Thomas

Ikusei: Nurture

A carefully curated anthology of haikus by various authors.

Weaving the Light

A women's appreciation anthology of essays, memoirs, poetry, and short stories by various authors.

9 781969 601002